THE BEGINNING AND THE END

ANTHONY EBUBECHUKWU ORJI

CONTENTS

Title Page   1

Copyright   2

The beginning and the end   7

The beginning of creation   8

Discussion with an atheist   10

Wisdom   12

The Time When Things Fell Apart   14

Evil On Earth After the Fall   15

The Time When Men Began To Multiply   17

The Time When Blacks Were Created   19

Foolishness and Wickedness   22

The Writer   25

The Time When Man Was Made A Clone Before the Devil   31

Time When A Man (the Writer) Was Made A Clone   34

Dreams   38

The Beginning of Creation   39

Things That God Created For His Pleasure   41

The Reason the Devil Wants Man To Taste The Pit (Hell)   43

Who is this woman (Abadidon)   45

The Time When Men were Included In Hell   49

The Name of the Creator   52

The Creation of the Devil 53

The Fall of Man 55

The Mystery of Regeneration 57

Destroying the Soul Particle in Hell 60

Regeneration of the Dead 62

The Mystery So Far 66

The Question 68

The Rapture 71

The Mystery of the Rapture 74

THE BEGINNING AND THE END

You are the one I am looking for! You are the one I am looking for! How can you look for me when I am already in the pit (hell)? How can you look for me when I am dining with the devil?

Oh no! Who are you looking for? I am looking for a man after my heart. Stop confusing me. How can you look for a man after your heart when the one after your heart is one that loves women Even though you are a merciful God. Why did you allow him to see you Even after committing murder and adultery? How can I explain all things to you seeing there are secrets with God?

What is the secret? What is the secret? The secret is that all were created by God but all are not equally loved by God. But why? Yes! How can a man (cain) kill his brother and was banished from the presence of God and another (david) killed a brother (uriah) and was forgiven even after sleeping with his wife (bathsheba)? Yes! You are God but I have some reservations, here are some of my reservation.

THE BEGINNING
OF CREATION

You were told that a man (Adam) was made from clay and a woman (Eve) was made from the rib of the man, then why are women still having complete ribs instead of just one rib if that is true that you removed a rib from the man and made woman?

Yes! I have the power to multiply things. Do you think I created the stars one by one? Not at all. How can I remove a rib from the man and made a woman with the same one rib? No! It is impossible, I had to multiply (mystery) the rib and I had to multiply the stars Even after creating one.

Yes! How can a man (white) produce a car and still want to go through the stress of making the car in a way that is energy demanding if not that such a man is unwise? Yes! He (whites) must first of all find a way of making his product less energy demanding so that at least he can produce more in lesser time yet still maintaining the quality of the cars produced.

Look I created man from dust and I made woman from his rib. How can a woman be compared to a man that was created from dust? Yes! A man may love his wife because he believes she was created from his rib but deep down in the man's heart he knows that it is not possible for a man (surgeon) to cut open his rib and from that rib make a woman although it is very impractical to think of that but very practical to believe .

DISCUSSION WITH AN ATHEIST

Atheist: How can man be created from dust when man came from nothing into something?

God: How can man be created from dust when man came from the third heaven into the world?

Theologian: God created man in his image and likeness.

Athiest: If man was created from the dust how come the whites cannot create man from dust since they have the power to make things that are beyond imagination?

God: How can man be created by whites when they are truly men and not spirits?

Theologian: I am getting lost in this discussion.

As I looked at man, I discovered that men may not want to believe they were recloned form the first man and his wife, Adam and Eve. As I looked at the first Adam, I discovered that he was truly created form dust but as I looked at another Adam (a black man), I discovered he was recloned. The Africa are recloned, whereas White men were created.

On Angels of light, they were created from a single stone except Lucifer who was created with multiple stones. African, were truly recloned from Adam although that was not mentioned in the scriptures. On Eve (a white woman), she was created but on the black woman she was recloned.

Looking at the mystery above, a black man may want to curse the writer but the writer does not know what he is about to write seeing he is not the one writing but the Holy Spirit through him, hence he writes without brainstorming . If he was the one writing, the devil will chain him but if he writes through the spirit(holy), the devil will die(mystery) because he(writer) is writing things of the third world when he is still in the first world (earth).

As I considered men under the surface of the sun, I discovered they had knowledge but lacked wisdom due to one reason or the other.

WISDOM

How can a man born of a woman look at the curves of a woman twice without being seduced by the devil to imagine evil in his hearts? How can man lust at a woman and still want to look at God? A theologian was very impatient with my writing seeing I wrote things that were not common to man. He asked if it was holy literature or just an ordinary book seeing there was no scriptural backing to my writing. On this, let's go on a scriptural exploration.

The book of Genesis

As I flipped through the book of genesis, I discovered it talked about the beginning of creation and as I flipped through page by page, I discovered that it was a mystery that a man may explain the bible by the standard of heaven. How can a man born of woman explain the bible by the standard of heaven?

Explanation of the book of Genesis

A man (Jehovah) created a beast (Lucifer) to be with him for eternity seeing other angels cannot come before the cloud of his glorious majesty because of his much power. The beast (Lucifer) was created with several stones so that he will be preserved before the one to whom all glory is due to, that is Jehovah.

The writer is not a Jehovah's witness lest man begins to ask why the continual use of the name "Jehovah". Yes! He (Jehovah) is the one that created all things and without him was nothing created that was created. Now Lucifer was specially created by him (Jehovah) although the Son and the Father are one, hence Lucifer was also created by the Son. Now if a man asks this question is it wrong? What is the name of the day God created man and if that day is special, why is man still living in filthiness?

Look, God created man on the sixth day although that day is a great day to the Son because it was the Son that created man but the Father and the Son are one, hence man was created by the Father.

Okay, what of the Holy Ghost, why are we (Father and Son) not writing him (Holy Ghost) Even in this mystery for man to know who he is. The Holy Ghost is not involved in either the creation of the beast (Lucifer) or man but was the one engineering the creation of both, hence he is also the Creator of the beast (Lucifer) and man. How can a man that brought the prototype of the design not mentioned in the one that made the car, then it will be evil.

The Holy Ghost

There is thunder in the sky! There is thunder in the sky! Looking at the sky to know what it was, I discovered that a spirit (Holy Ghost) was passing through. How can thunder strike because God (Holy Ghost) was passing through? Yes! He is not all that friendly although merciful. Oh no! No wonder he is in charge of the fire that chastises the devil. No wonder he is in charge of the thunder in the sky and when he thunders, his mercy endures forever if not man (flesh) that just raped a woman supposed to be struck dead by the thunder. If not a man that stole was supposed to be struck dead by the thunder. If not a woman (widow) that sleeps around supposed to be struck dead. If not a man that went to a native doctor was supposed to be struck dead.

THE TIME WHEN THINGS FELL APART

Things fell apart at the Garden of Eden. Things fell apart when man (Eve) disobeyed God and death reigned on earth. Things fell apart when the man wanted to be as wise as God. Things fell apart when the devil regenerated into a serpent and the man lost his place before God.

How can a woman allow a man (devil) to rape (deceive) her even before her husband (God)? Yes! The devil raped (deceived) man before his husband (God). As I looked at the creation of man, I discovered that man may be seen as the weakest thing after the fall seeing that man is now controlled by the devil. Yes! The devil had control of man immediately after the fall.

Look at the devil cursing the writer because of what he is writing, he knows that no man under the sun would write things he does not know but the writer is writing things (spiritual) he does not know through the Holy Spirit. How can a man (devil) curse another man (writer) if not that the man (writer) is also spirit although covered with the flesh?

As I looked at the beginning of creation, tears (blood) tickled down my chin (holy). As I looked at the beginning of creation, I discovered that eternity will not forgive the devil for using man as a tool to develop evil on earth.

EVIL ON EARTH AFTER THE FALL

Who taught man that rings are to be worn on the body? Who taught man how to paint to change the way I created them? Who taught man that strong drink is good to be taken? Who taught man how to bath the dead? Who taught man how to fornicate? Who taught man adultery? Who taught man lies? Who taught man murder either through abortion or killing? Who taught man how to steal? Who taught man how to change the way I created them into something else?

As I looked at the earth, I discovered that man has corrupted his way upon the earth and it repented me for creating man. Yes! How can a man want to know (evil) an angel that was sent to warn them of their evil? How can a man want to know (evil) an angel if not that that generation was highly controlled by the devil? Yes! It is a generation that was controlled by the devil seeing it is a generation that so committed evil that God had to send his angels in form of flesh to preach the everlasting gospel to them before the end (destruction). But they neglected the bidding of the angels due to their much evil and not just that they wanted to know the angels. How can such a generation escape from the wrath of God if not that the devil is truly the one controlling that generation?

Another man just raped a daughter of a great man (Jacob) due to the greed of the flesh. Yes! Another man just committed suicide because he betrayed his master (Jesus). Another man (Amon) just slept with his half-sister (Tamar). Another man (Achan) disobeyed God and stole of the accursed things and because of that brought grievous sin upon the children of Israel. Another man (Er) was slain by God because of his wickedness. Another man (Samson) neglected the bidding of God in his life and went after harlots. Another man (Cain) slew his brother (Abel) because of envy and jealousy. Another man(Uriah) was killed by a servant of God (David) due to wickedness.

As I looked at the evil on earth, it repented God that he created man. How can a man that was created in the image and likeness of God go for transgender if not that man is now controlled by the devil? How can man created in the image and likeness of God go for abortion if not that they are controlled by the devil? How can man created in the image and likeness of God go for rituals if not that they are controlled by the devil? How can man (cultist) be used by the devil in causing accidents if not that man has truly been cheated by the devil? As I looked at the evil on earth, tears (blood) tickled down my chin.

THE TIME WHEN MEN BEGAN TO MULTIPLY

The time men (mortals) began to multiply is in the word (bible). It was in the word that a generation multiplied and they also multiplied their evil on earth. It repented God that he made man on earth. How can man corrupt his ways on earth? How can beast be judged (destroyed) by the lord in that generation. As I (Christ) looked at the earth, I discovered that eternity will not forgive man for corrupting his ways upon the earth. Yes! How can man be so corrupt to the extent he wants to enter into an affair with the angels of the Most High who brought the Everlasting gospel during the time of Lot in Sodom.

How can a man be so evil to kill his brother (Abel) just because of envy? How can a man be so evil that he (Er) was slain by God due to his wickedness? How can men be so evil to the extent envy and jealousy led them into selling their brother (Joseph)? How can men be so evil that they came together to build a city and tower as high as heaven, if not out of foolishness? How can a man (Judas Iscariot) sell his master because of thirty pieces of silver? How can a man bring a curse on everyone due to disobedience? How can a man enter into a covenant with the devil through jewelries? How can a man be so evil that he (Ahab) killed another man (Naboth) and collected his Father's possession? How can a man be so evil that he (Jeroboam) seduced the children of Israel into worshipping idols just because he did not want to lose the loyalty of the children of Israel to the king of Judah (Rehoboam)?

How can humanity be this evil that they reviled their Creator on the cross telling him to come down from the cross if he was truly what he claimed he was? How can men be so evil to use (the evil of demons) the cloth of their Creator in casting lots? How can men be so evil that they placed thorns upon the head of their Creator? How can men (the Pharisees) be so evil that they persecuted the apostles not to preach about Christ?

THE TIME WHEN BLACKS WERE CREATED

As I looked at the beginning of creation, I discovered that the word "created" may be used for the blacks although it is not apt to use such words seeing that blacks (Africans) were truly "recloned" from Adam (blacks) and Eve (blacks). Yes! It is not very easy to look at a creature and tell him that he was not created but recloned. How can a man(Jehovah) create Adam (white) and Eve (white) and Adam (black) and Eve(black) but at the end, it was only Adam (white) and Eve (white) that was recognized in the scripture. Yes! It is a mystery that it was only Adam (white) and Eve (white) that was recognized seeing that it is not too good to talk about the mystery of the creation of the blacks (Africans). Yes! The blacks may not know why they are called blacks by the white except they see the mystery of their creation.

The Mystery of the Creation of the Blacks

How can God create a man and a woman (white) and another man and woman (black) but in the end, he (Jehovah) only mentioned the white and not the black. Yes! Jehovah is the Creator of man and spirits. He is the Creator of the day (white) and the night (black). He is the Creator of holy spirits and evil spirits. He is the Creator of the moon (black) and the sun (white). He is the Creator of giants and dwarfs. He is the Creator of the forces of light (white) and the forces of darkness (black). He is the Creator of angels of light (white) and angels of darkness (blacks). He is the Creator of heaven (white) and hell (black). He is the Creator of man (white) when he was in the region that is of light and the Creator of blacks when he was in the region that cannot be mentioned. He (Jehovah) is the Creator of the tree of life (white) and the tree of the knowledge of good and evil (black).

He is the Creator of heaven (white) and earth (neither white nor black). He (Jehovah) is the Creator of spirit (white) and spirit (beast- that is neither of light nor darkness). He (Jehovah) is the Creator of things (soul) that is neither of light nor of darkness. He is the Creator of light (gospel) and he is the one that created the one (devil) that has made dark things (fornication, mastur-bation, alcoholism, worldly music, adultery, reveling, gambling, robbery, pornography). He (Jehovah) is the one that created the blacks (Africans) thousands of years ago in a region that is beyond human reasoning.

How can God create the "blacks" and then make them some-how inferior to the whites? He (Jehovah) made them lower in "thoughts", actions (mysteries) to the whites. How can a man(black) think of making another die a painful death if not that that man is truly "black"? How can a man (black) be angry that his brother that was born by the same mother succeeds if not that he is truly black? The whites may be angry but with time they will become humbled and repent. How can a man (black) sleep with his brother's wife and at the same time sleep with his brother's daughters if not that he is truly black although for the whites they may do more than that due to foolishness? For the blacks, they may do that due to wickedness. How can a man (black) sleep with a madwoman just because he wants to make money (filthy) if not that he (black) is truly a black man? How can a man (black) sleep with a day old child if not that he (a black man) is truly black although a white man may do that out of foolishness; a black man will do that out of wickedness.

FOOLISHNESS AND WICKEDNESS

As I looked at the two words, I was tempted to ask if such words should be used for man (white and black). An evil being walked up to me and told me if he were to say, I will not be allowed to write about these two words seeing I (the writer) have exhibited both when I have not known God.

Oh no! Lucifer, were you not the one that made him (writer) exhibited such words (foolishness and wickedness) through your seduction on him (writer). Yes! Lucifer you have seduced men (black and white) into becoming what God did not intend for them. You (Lucifer) have seduced even the whites into evil on earth more than the blacks. You (Lucifer) have seduced the blacks into becoming more evil just as you were cursed (darkness). You have seduced aliens (transgender) into becoming hermaphrodite when God did not make them so.

You have seduced porn actors into spreading devilish evangelism through your evil on them. You (Lucifer) have made man hate the things of God through your seduction on them. You have made women hate the way I created them through your seduction on them. You have made women hop from one bed to another because of your seduction on them. You have made women hate their natural hair because of your seduction on them. You (Lucifer) have made women hate the heavenly coloured lips because of your seduction on them. You have made women hate the heavenly coloured fingernails because of your seduction on them. You have made women hate their skin colour because of your seduction on them. You have made women hate the eyelashes I (Christ) gave them because of your seduction on them. You have made women hate the genital I gave them because of your seduction on them. How could you (Lucifer) be so wicked to seduce the creation of God into changing their genitals if not that you are evil? You have made man a tool in your hands.

As I looked at the word "foolishness", I discovered that man (whites) are truly foolish because of the level of intelligence I (Jehovah) created them with. Yes! I (Jehovah) created them with brains that are not easily gotten. Yes! The whites are more in knowledge than blacks. But the blacks, I (Jehovah) created their skin to be more resistant to the harsh weather conditions of the environment. Oh no! How can I (Jehovah) create the whites (men of knowledge) and in the end the devil uses them as a tool.

Whites As a Tool In the Devil's Hand

I (Jehovah) regretted giving you (whites) the knowledge that supersedes most knowledge! I (Jehovah) regret giving you (whites) the knowledge you (whites) are using against me (Jehovah). I (Jehovah) regret giving you much knowledge. I (Jehovah) regret giving you the ability to discover new things. I (Jehovah) regret giving you the ability to invent new things. I (Jehovah) regret giving you (whites) the ability to be different in all spheres of life above the blacks. I regret giving you (whites) the ability to discover new things even things hidden from an ordinary man (blacks).

Blacks As An Ordinary Man

How can I (Jehovah) call "blacks" an ordinary man? How can I (Jehovah) call blacks ordinary men? Yes! I (Jehovah) created the blacks as though they were not as important as the whites.

Yes! The writer is a black man from a West African country. How can a man (a black man) write against himself if not that a spirit (holy) is writing through him?

As I looked at the writer, I discovered it will take the whites (men of knowledge) eternity to go into the lab and discover who is writing through the writer. How can a man (the writer) write without brainstorming? How can a man write without cancellation? How can a man write without thinking about what he wants to write?

THE WRITER

The writer is a beast! The writer is a beast! The writer is not human! The writer is not human! The writer is supernatural! The writer is not an ordinary man! The writer is not an ordinary man! The writer was given a rare gift by the Creator! The writer was given a rare gift by the Creator! The writer is a clone of the heavenly beast!

The writer is not going to eat from the tree of life! The writer is not going to eat from the tree of life! The tree of life is for overcomers to eat so that they will not die and hence live with the Creator for eternity. The writer is spirit, all spirit does not need the tree of life to live for eternity. All spirits were created with stones but the writer was cloned from a heavenly beast that was created with stone. The writer cannot be seen eye to eye in spirit without the other spirit not feeling like running away seeing that the writer in spirit can command the "day" to be night and night to be day although, in the spiritual realm, it is either day (heavenly) or night (hell). But no man knows that we also have neither light (day) nor darkness(night) except if the reader has read from the books written by the author.

Yes! We have creatures that are neither light nor of darkness and we have regions that are neither light nor of darkness. We have things (souls) that are neither of light nor of darkness and we have spirits (beasts) that are neither of light nor of darkness. We have creatures that are neither of light nor of darkness but are more of darkness than of light. An example of such creature is the water spirits although it is not too good to call them spirit seeing they are half-human and half-spirit.

Yes! Merman and mermaid are neither of light nor of darkness but are more of darkness than of light. A theologian walked up to me and asked me if I am "insane" but I (writer) looked at him and laughed seeing he does not know that his soul is neither of light nor of darkness. Anything he (theologian) gives it, it will take that shape. If the theologian gives his soul light (holy literature, gospel music, Christian magazines, Christian tracts) his soul (neither of light nor darkness) will adopt the position of light and if he (theologian) gives his soul (neither of light nor darkness) darkness (worldly music, porn, fornication, gambling, alcoholism, masturbation, smoking, reveling, lesbianism, homosexually, bestiality, necrophilia, adultery, idolatry, sorcery, cultism, witchcraft, lies, cheating) his soul will adopt the position of darkness.

As I looked into the creation of God. I discovered that the bible did not talk much of water spirits (merman and mermaid) except when Christ was walking on the sea and his disciples shouted that he was a ghost. As I looked into the creation of God, I discovered that it will take man (both white and black) eternity to know the mystery of the creation of God.

As I looked into the hearts of the earth (ocean and sea), I discovered life(evil) are existing in the water bodies. As I looked at the man (white and black), I discovered that man is a little foolish about how to live in the flesh. As I looked at a man (false prophet) about to sacrifice to the water spirits, I discovered that he was just too foolish to be called a man of God seeing he (false prophet) has succeeded in tying those (men and women) that patronizes him seeking for false miracles everywhere. As I looked at him, I discovered he was too foolish for my liking seeing he had entered into a covenant with the water spirits unknowingly.

As I considered the woman patronising him wanting to bath, I discovered she was a woman that was looking for a child. I discovered she does not know that by allowing the prophet bath her at the riverside, she has entered into a covenant with the marine world. As I looked at the items brought by the woman, I discovered they were marine (spiritual) items - items that were neither of light nor of darkness. As I looked at one of the items (candle), I discovered it is a normal product gotten from animal fats and plant but the spiritual implication attached to it is not an easy one. If one looks at the candlestick, it was created by the Most High that is to say it is a product of God's creativity. If a black candle (darkness) and a white candle are melted and mixed, the white candle and the black candle will have no difference when it is cooled that is why the merman and mermaid require either white or black candle from their victims through the false prophet. But for the red candles, it is for the ogbonis. Now if the water spirits (merman and mermaid) likes white candles and the ogbonis like red candles, is there any difference in both? Yes! There is a great difference in both. The difference is that one is of light and the other (red) is of darkness. One is white and the other red (danger) but both are all having spiritual implications provided the victim is not burning the candle to light the house but for prayers.

Immediately the person starts praying, the marine spirits will cover the general atmosphere where the person is praying so that his prayer will not leave an inch above the ceiling of his building. But if the person is a sinner then there is no need because his prayer is already of an offensive odour before God. But come to think of it, candle is not bad in general but it is the motive behind it. The most dangerous of candles are black candles, they are demonic and has demonic implications when it is burnt either to lighten the house or for demonic incantation by devilish spiritualists.

Black candles are used in the spiritual realm to monitor the spirits of one (sinners) living on earth especially if a person wants to kill his fellow, he uses a black candle. What he needs to do is just to write the person's name on a clean white sheet of paper and as the candle is burning, the drop out is used in closing up the name that was written upon the white sheet and after that, that person is a dead man if he is a sinner except by the mercy of God. If one wants to differentiate white candles and black candles by the power of the Holy Ghost it will take a lot of work.

Now if a man takes a white candle and burn it, you will observe that the candle is melting and the wick is also burning with the wax. If the candle reaches a certain point, it will become very small to the extent that the wick is almost burnt yet the candle will still be burning. Now if the candle is almost about to finish, what happens is that the wick becomes a little smaller while the wax continues melting, at about the point of finishing, one will observe that the candle is smaller than the light that is radiating only for the light to go out without the candle wax finishing at the same time with it. If one takes the remaining candle and melt it , one will observe that the wick that was remaining is not the same as the remaining wax. But what is the reason behind this? The reason behind this is that when one takes a drop of a candle from a melting pan and then the same person takes another candle (red) from another pan, if the pan is white (earthen), one will observe that the red candle mixes with the earthen pan.

Okay! What is all this about? It is about light and darkness. The marine spirits (merman and mermaid) like white candles because of the light emanating from them but they hate the light because they are neither light nor darkness. But why are the marine spirits (merman and mermaid) neither light nor darkness? Come to think of it, if a man (clay) dies, he will be buried in the grave, immediately that man is laid down into the earth (earthen pan), if the man is a righteous and holy man (light), he (born again) will not mix with the earth (hell) but if the man is a sinner, immediately he (sinner) is laid into the earth (red), he (sinner) will mix with the earth (hell). Hence, the man (sinner) decays and mixes with the earth because he (sinner) is earthly (worldly). Likewise, marine spirits (merman and mermaid) are neither of light nor of darkness, yet they (merman and mermaid) are of darkness since they are the servant of the devil (darkness).

Another item that is neither of light nor of darkness is egg. An egg is neither evil nor good if one takes an egg that is freshly laid by a chicken and boil it, if it is properly boiled, you will observe that the outer part is white while the inner part is black. The marine spirits (merman and mermaid) are neither of light nor of darkness hence the marine spirits need eggs as a sacrificial item from men (victims).

Another items so much needed by the marine world from their victims is "red cloth". At the beginning of creation, red is a symbol of authority because of it attractive nature and not only that, it is used as a spiritual atonement for the Passover feast by the Jews. Okay! What is the meaning of spiritual atonement? Is that whenever a woman is menstruating and she is spiritually unclean, she is normally given a red cloth to wear so that peradventure she bleeds out, she will not easily be noticed. So red has some spiritual significance. Likewise when the angel of death was passing through the land of Egypt during the Passover night, the angel (angel of death) was given a signal not to go into where he (angel of death) sees red but he (angel of death) can go where there were other colours. So, the blood of a lamb was used as an atonement that night to save the firstborn of Israel from death. But if one looks at the scripture, one will observe that Rahab used a red cloth as a signal to the children when they were about to attack the land of Jericho but due to the covenant which Rahab entered with the children of Israel, she was preserved by that signal. So, red has spiritual significance - spiritually it means covenant by blood but physically it means danger hence making both interwoven and separate.

Marine spirits (merman and mermaid) normally request red cloth from their foolish victims because anytime they come with red cloth, it means that they have brought the symbol of their authority which is the blood of the Passover which is supposed to be with them to their opponents and as such they have allowed the marine spirits (merman and mermaid) to use their authority against them. Hence, when they bring the red cloth as a sacrificial item, they are made to remove the power that signifies "do not touch" on them, hence making them prone to marine manipulation. They have also entered into a covenant with the marine world unknowingly, except if they are delivered by the blood of the lamb, that is when the marine spirits (merman and mermaid) will succumb from tormenting such spiritually especially through dreams.

Looking at the whole mysteries above, a white man will truly go into the lab to perform such research to know what the writer wrote about "candle" if it is correct but a black man will only read and take it to either be true or false depending on his flesh (mysteries of mysteries) or on his mind (mysteries of mysteries) or finally his will (mysteries).

Yes! The writer cannot speak of himself except by the Holy Ghost. The writer cannot speak of himself except the devil is chained. The writer cannot speak of himself except if Christ permits it. The writer cannot speak of himself except Christ chain the power of darkness. The writer cannot speak of himself except Christ allow him (the beast/writer) to speak. The writer cannot speak of himself except Christ make the devil bow to the power in him. The writer cannot speak of himself except Christ make him a clone that cannot be chained. How can a man born of a woman understand what it means for God to make a man (writer) a clone that cannot be chained? If any man has understanding then let him wait don't read further and try to explain it in the shallowness of his heart.

THE TIME WHEN MAN WAS MADE A CLONE BEFORE THE DEVIL

L ook I (Jehovah) have the power to write things that even if a million white men are put inside a room given a million times to unravel such a question but will not be able to. Okay! Let me start by asking:

Question 1. How can a man (the devil) that was told that his wife (Abadidon) is about to deliver feels very happy instead of him running here and there to look for what his wife will need for her delivery and then decided to wait for the wife to put to birth and immediately strangle her babies just because of the wickedness of his heart? Satan! How come you who was supposed to at least pity those children (damned souls) born to you, decided to torment them with the trident God (Jehovah) gave to you. Are you this foolish! Are you this foolish!

Look at the write up above, one will want to ask that the writer did not answer the first question which was "I (Christ) made him(writer) a clone that cannot be chained". Oh no! How can a man answer such a question? Mr writer, are you a human being or a spirit being (beast)?

You are half man and half spirit. But how can a man (the writer) be half man and half spirit when even the whites (men of knowledge) cannot explain the mysteries of some terms in plain language. I assembled the whites and I asked them a simple question, and the question goes like this:

Can man explain in plain language what happens when a man dies and after a few minutes the man is seen in another state either buying or selling or even marrying? Mr writer please stop confusing those men you placed inside the room for them to answer your question. You assumed that a million white men were placed inside a room and you have asked them series of questions that most intelligent professors cannot unravel. But who is talking about professors here, when a professor is just educated to either write or to say what he knows as a result of excessive reading but here is a man (writer) that writes things that are not common to man.

Okay! I want to ask another question it is: how can a man explain Trinity in plain language? As I wrote " Trinity" a holy being walked up to me and told me that all the professors that were inside that room would at least be happy that I have asked a question that is common to man and that can be easily answered. The first professor that was inside the room said that there is nothing like "Trinity" that God is one but another professor inside the room looked at me and told me that it is the God head that is, God the Father, God the Son and God the Holy Spirit.

As the professor wrote Holy Spirit, I was tempted to laugh inside the room. But why the laughter? Why the laughter? Yes, it is a mystery that a man (writer/beast) would explain the scripture by the standard of heaven. The professors that were inside the building were almost angry seeing that they were all seeing me (writer) as one that is proud. Oh no! Professors I know you are truly seeing me as one that is proud but I am not . How can I (writer) be proud when I am not the one writing ? Yes, it is the Holy Ghost that is writing through me. Okay! If I ask another question, you will get more confused.

At the last expression, all the professors raised their hands that they can answer the last question. Among them was one that recently lost his wife through murder. Looking at the word "murder", I discovered that the word is not just an ordinary word but one that is highly spiritual. How can murder be a word that is highly spiritual? Yes! Murder is associated with a spirit (evil of demons) that is highly demonic.

What is the difference between demonic and Satanic? I asked, the professors were now angry and one almost did something that provoked me. Yes! Professor you are to raise your hands when you have something bothering your mind and then you should raise your hands not just by you showing a sad expression on your face.

Again I reconsidered the question that was asked, I discovered it is only a man that is supernatural that can answer such a question. Who is the man? Who is the man? As I looked at the professors, I discovered they were very angry with me seeing that they thought I was making a fool of them but it is not so professors, I repeat, it is not so.

TIME WHEN A MAN (THE WRITER) WAS MADE A CLONE

The time when the man (writer) was made a clone is in this new generation. Yes! How can a man be made a clone if not that he is not an ordinary man? Yes! The man (writer) is not an ordinary man, he has the power (spirits of spirits) to pray and arrows (spiritual) are pulled from the third heaven into the pit (hell). Yes! If I see another man (flesh) that can do that I (Jehovah) will strike him dead. Yes! No man under the surface of the sun is given that kind of power. Okay! This is what it means for a man (writer) to pray and arrows (spiritual) are drawn from the third heaven into the pit (hell).

The mystery

The mystery of the creation of the beast (writer) cannot be explained in plain language the reason being that the mystery is a mystery beyond spirits. Oh no! How can the mystery be beyond spirits? Yes! The beast (writer) has the power to command things spiritually to things physically. Now if I ask a man a question, human beings will not believe. The question goes like this: a man (writer) was born through regeneration and another man was born through degeneration what is the difference between these two?

Now the first child born through regeneration is a terror to the kingdom of darkness but the other one born through degeneration is a terror to the kingdom of light. Oh no! How can a man born of a woman understand what Jehovah is saying?

Regeneration

What is regeneration? What is regeneration? It is the ability to exist in a state that is different from the normal state. What is the state? What is the state? How can a man born of a woman understand regeneration if not that that man is a clone? Yes! For a man to be a clone, it means that such a man has a mirror image. What is the mirror image? The mirror image of a man is the real image of a man in a state that is beyond human reasoning. Okay! This is what it means to clone a man that is still alive.

Cloning

Who invented you (cloning)? Who invented you (cloning)? As I asked the question, I was told that a man that just died is about to undergo judgment. Looking at the judgment, I discovered that the man was going to weep for eternity in the pit (hell). Yes! The man lived a life of filthiness in the flesh. He lived watching pornography and he was a masturbator. How can a man that watches porn and also a masturbator enter into the kingdom of light?

No! It is not possible for a man that has defilement all over his garments to see God. Oh no! Now, this is what happens when a man (sinner) dies. Immediately a man dies, the devil will release evil spirits into where the person's corpse is lying and with time the person (soul) will observe that he is getting weaker along the judgment queue as he is proceeding to the angels that judges. As the person (soul) begins to move steadily, he will observe that he is getting weaker and weaker as he goes along the judgment queue. But with time, he will observe that he is getting weaker and weaker as he goes along the judgment queue the reason is that the person died as a sinner.

As I looked at humanity, I discovered they will immediately be afraid if their spiritual eyes are opened to what the devil is doing in the region of darkness.

Again as I looked at a man, I discovered he does not know that the devil has his clone. Foolish man you died as a fornicator and a fornicator is a man that has a clone with the devil and through the clone, the devil will keep on making him or she fornicates anytime he wishes. Yes! The devil has clones of all sinners in the world whether humanity believes it or not. Immediately a man dies, he will be given a final judgment "depart ye worker of iniquity" as it is happening, the devil will immediately prepare a special place for such a man to burn for eternity while the clone of the man will be used to torment him forever in the pit (hell).

But how can the devil be this evil to use the clone of a man (damned soul) against him? Okay! The devil will be exposed properly in this book.

Cloning of the dead

Look at the devil cursing the writer (beast)! Look at the devil cursing the writer! As I looked into a building (darkest region), I discovered that the devil was just too wicked for my(holy) liking seeing he has succeeded in making the creation of God act foolishly!

Fools

A fool is a man that does not want to eat after death. A fool is a man that doesn't want to sleep after death. A fool is a man that hates living seeing those in the pit are called dead men.

<u>Dead men</u>

Dead men are damned souls in the pit (hell). Dead men are fallen angels, dead men are "death". Dead men are evil spirits. How can a man born of a woman look at the curves of a woman and expect the devil to spare his eyes? How can a man born of a woman look at filthy pictures and expect to sleep again if he mistakenly dies in such filth?

Look, dead men are human who died without repentance on earth and were either not regenerated or sent back to their bodies (corpse) to wake up again on earth. Dead men cannot see God except through dreams.

DREAMS

How can one inside the pit (hell) dream if it is not a falasy! Yes! Dead men can only see Jehovah through dreams.

Is there sleep in the pit (hell)? The answer is a very big no. Then how can dreams be attached to the damned that cannot close their eyes spiritually? Oh no! Dead men can only dream by their already polluted spirits. Yes! The spirit of a dead man (damned) is before God (Jehovah) seeing he is the Father of all spirits (holy) and (evil) and the Father of all flesh both (holy) and (evil). Oh no! How can the spirit of a man (damned) that died to be before God (Jehovah) if not that such a man deserves to be killed – impossible. But how can a man that is already doomed be killed again?

Killing a damned soul

Okay! A damned soul cannot exist just like a single soul but like a soul that has an outer covering. What is the outer covering? The outer covering of a soul is the spirit that was returned to the Creator (Jehovah). Okay! What if the spirit were to be on earth, what will it be called? It will be called the "spirit of the dead". Oh no! I think it is time to consult my bible seeing all this while I have been writing without consulting my bible.

THE BEGINNING OF CREATION

The beginning of creation was when God said let there be light and there was light. The beginning of creation was when God created the things that were not to things that are. The beginning of creation was when the forces of light were empowered to do things beyond human reasoning. The beginning of creation was when the forces of light (Holy-Spirit) was given power over the forces of darkness. The beginning of creation was when things fell apart (the great tribulation). The beginning of creation was when God had to drive away Lucifer from his presence. The beginning of creation was when Adam and Eve were created although Eve was not created but was recloned from Adam using just a tiny piece (rib) from Adam. The beginning of creation was when time (mysteries) was set into eternity. The beginning of creation was when the serpent was given a rare deceptive (crafty) mechanism above all animals created. The beginning of creation was when Adam was given the breath of life by God.

The time When Men Began To Multiply

A man (Abraham) was instructed by God to leave his Father's house to a land he knew not but with faith he left all temporal comfort to the land. As I looked at man, I discovered that man was truly foolish seeing that man really want to be like his Creator although man was like his Creator in the flesh but the devil been so wise regenerated into a serpent and deceived man. Man was told if he(she) eats from the tree of knowledge of good and evil, he will become as wise as his Creator. The devil is very intelligent and knows once man eats, he will become like the devil knowing good and evil.

Yes! Man became like the devil seeing that when the devil was before me, he was like me but immediately the spirit of pride defeated him in paradise, he became like the god of darkness knowing good and evil likewise he has to seduce man into being like him. As I looked at a man (Cain), I discovered he was the first man to taste hell, he was the first man to murder on earth although we have creatures (blacks) that were recloned and existed on various parts of the earth. It was a mystery that death reigned through the first Adam (black- recloned) and the first Eve (black-recloned).

Okay! Consider the fall of man at the Garden of Eden, one will say that it was not good that God (Jehovah) allowed Adam (white) and Eve (white) to fall. Let us expose some mysteries that are beyond human reasoning.

The Mystery

God created all things for his pleasure (mysteries). God almighty created all things for his pleasure (mysteries). God created all things for his pleasure.

THINGS THAT GOD CREATED FOR HIS PLEASURE

God (Jehovah) created both forces of light and darkness for his glory. God created giants that Even the whites (men of knowledge) do not know the planet they existed on. God created dwarfs for his pleasure. God created the stars for his glory. God created the sun (mysteries) for his glory. God created the marine spirits (merman and mermaid) for his glory. God created spirits of spirits (powers) for his glorious majesty. God created Lucifer for his glorious worship although after the fall Lucifer became recloned to the devil and after man (Adam and Eve) fell at the Garden of Eden, the devil was recloned and he became Satan (a tormentor). Immediately man (Adam and Eve) fell at the Garden of Eden, Jehovah gave Satan instruments of torments to torment damned souls that failed to serve him while on earth. God (Jehovah) created angels (both of light and darkness) for his glorious worship but immediately after the fall angels of light were separated from angels of darkness. God created the water bodies for his glorious majesty. God created things that fly for his glorious majesty. God created all things on earth for his glorious majesty.

As I looked at Adam (white) and Eve (white), I discovered that they are just too foolish not to know that they were like gods. Oh no! How can flesh be like gods if not that they are covered by the power of the Godhead through his anointing? Yes! They were like gods before the fall but immediately they disobeyed God, they became like the devil (knowing good and evil). Yes! Immediately man (Adam and Eve) fell in the garden, they became like the devil in knowledge hence man became wise (evil) like the devil and man lost his place before God.

As I looked at a man (writer) writing, I discovered he has a very, very rare gift. How can a man write things that men under the surface of the sun do not know? As I considered the beginning of creation, I discovered that it will take men eternity to understand the reason the devil wants all humanity to taste the pit (hell).

THE REASON THE DEVIL WANTS MAN TO TASTE THE PIT (HELL)

As I looked into the future (backward), I discovered that it is not going to be easy with any man that died without Christ. As I looked at the future (backward), I discovered that it will take men eternity to know why the devil wants man to taste hell. As I looked at the future (backward), I discovered that the devil was not happy with the way he was chased from the third heaven without prior warning. As I looked at the devil, I discovered that he was too crafty to be using humanity as a tool in his hands. As I looked at the beginning of creation, I discovered that the devil would have wished that Lucifer was present the day I created man.

Oh no! I (Jehovah) am God and I know that Lucifer would betray me in time (mystery) to come hence I had to send him on an errand (spiritually) when I wanted to create man. As I looked at another most powerful angel, I discovered she was an angel that was feared (mysteries) because of the stone that was used in creating her. As I looked at her (Abadidon), I discovered that her name before the fall was Medelene but after the fall her name changed to Abadidon just like Lucifer was changed to the devil. As I looked at the woman (Abadidon), I discovered that she was too evil to be used again as she was one time an angel of light. How can a woman (Abadidon) be this evil to cause millions and millions of souls (polluted) to cry for eternity? How can a woman (Abadidon) be so evil that she is seen as the queen of heaven? How can a woman (Abadidon) be so evil that she will Even seduce (evil of demon) the disciples of Jesus into committing suicide? How can a woman (Abadidon) be so evil that she will seduce the disciple of Jesus (Peter) into denying his master? How can a woman (Abadidon) seduce the wife of Potiphar into committing adultery (false)? How can a woman (Abadidon) seduce a great man (Samson) into committing fornication with a harlot (Delilah)? How can a woman (Abadidon) seduce Ananias and Sapphira into lying against the Holy Ghost? How can a woman (Abadidon) seduce Amon into forcing his half-sister (Tamar) to sleep with her?

Oh no! Abadidon is in charge of fornication, adultery, masturbation, lies, idolatry, suicide, murder (abortion). As I looked into the future (backward), I discovered that it will not be easy with humanity due to the creation of that woman (Abadidon).

WHO IS THIS WOMAN (ABADIDON)

Hey! Look at a woman (Abadidon) that is never tired watching pornography (physically)? Look at a woman that is never tired of fornicating with the devil to make the creation of God (humanity) have an uncontrollable urge for sex. Look at a woman that has seduced apostles, prophets, evangelists, teachers, pastors, and bishops into falling into the sin of fornication, adultery, masturbation, lies, pornography, idolatry, murder(abortion). Look at a woman (Abadidon) that almost made a great servant of God (David) miss heaven because of the love(false) of women. Look at a woman (Abadidon) that has rendered many homes useless through the quest to satisfy falsely the flesh through sex. Look at a woman (Abadidon) that has rendered many genitals useless through abortion. Look at a woman (Abadidon) that has rendered many women useless through their false outward appearance. Look at a woman (Abadidon) that have succeeded in changing the appearance of the creation of God. Look at a woman (Abadidon) that has succeeded in making women love(false) fornication. Look at a woman (Abadidon) that has made women hate the way Christ created them. Look at a woman (Abadidon) that has made women and millions of them cry in the pit (hell) because of her deception on them.

As I flipped through the bible, I discovered that the woman (Abadidon) was mentioned in a dark word. As I flipped through the book of Revelation, I discovered that it will take the whites (men of knowledge) eternity to truly know who this woman (Abadidon) was seeing she had succeeded in changing the whites into what I did not create them.

Whites

Whites! Whites! Did I (Christ) create you so special that the blacks are envious of you? Whites! Whites! Why have you allowed this woman (Abadidon) to gain upper hands over you? Whites! Whites! I (Christ) gave you beautiful hair just like the hair of flock of goats that appear from mount Gilead (Song of Solomon 4:1), I gave you (whites) eyes like that of the fish pools in Heshbon (Song of Solomon 7:4), the nose I (Christ) gave you (whites) is like that of the tower of Lebanon which looketh toward Damascus and the smell of your nose like apples (Song of Solomon 7: 8b). I gave thy women breasts as the clusters of the vine. I (Christ) gave you (whites) teeth like the flock of sheep that are Even shorn that came up from the washing where of everyone bear twins, and none is barren among them (Song of Solomon 6:6). I (Christ) made thee (whites) as fair as the moon, clear as the sun (Song of Solomon 6:10b).

Oh whites! Why have you allowed Abadidon to cheat you seeing she has also changed your appearance through her filthy outward appearance. She (Abadidon/ queen of demons) has made you believe the hair I gave you is not good enough hence covering the hair I (Christ) gave you thousands of years ago with false hair (artificial, attachment, weave on). She(Abadidon) has made you detest the heavenly eyelashes I gave you thousands of years and you are covering it with a false one from the devil. She has made you detest the heavenly coloured lips and change it with a false one (lipsticks- red yellow, brown, black). She has made you detest the heavenly coloured fingernails I (Christ) gave you thousands of years ago and covering it with a false one - artificial.

How could man be this wicked? How could man be this evil? As I (Christ) looked at the beginning of creation, I (Christ) discovered that the devil has personalities just like God. Yes! There are mysteries that are beyond human reasoning. There are mysteries that are sealed from the foundation of the world. How can a man write things that Even the best theologian in the world does not know if not that that man is supernaturally created. Yes! As I looked at the devil, I discovered he was not happy the way I (Christ) recloned him from Lucifer seeing that Lucifer was once created with rare stones (Ezekiel 28:13). The devil was recloned from Lucifer seeing that he was changed by a great mysterious power of Jehovah into what man would call a disgusting creature. Yes! The devil is disgusting since he was supposed to be called the last creature to be recloned by Jehovah after the fall of Lucifer but man later fell in the Garden of Eden and the devil became recloned to Satan.

Satan is the last creature to be recloned by Jehovah because of the great evil that was liberated immediately man fell at the Garden of Eden. Satan became highly empowered to torment damned souls that will fail to serve God on earth. Yes! Jehovah gave Satan instruments of torment to afflict souls that will fail to serve him on earth after death - as many as will not allow Christ reign in their life.

Yes! The devil is a deceiver and Satan is a tormentor. Lucifer is highly crafty but Lucifer cannot be in the region of darkness. Yes! Lucifer cannot be in the region of darkness because he was created in the region of light. Lucifer cannot be in light because he was banished from the presence of God. Lucifer cannot be in darkness because he was called Son of the morning. The devil cannot be in light because he was recloned in a region that was neither of light nor darkness. Satan cannot be in light because he was recloned after man (Adam and Eve) fell at the Garden of Eden. Man cannot be in light because he was banished from the presence of God after the fall. Man cannot be in darkness because he was created in a region that was neither of light nor darkness. Man cannot be in darkness because he was created with clay. Man cannot be in hell because man is truly flesh and not a soul. Man cannot be in hell because man cannot choose where to be after death. Man cannot be in hell because hell was created for the devil and his agents.

THE TIME WHEN MEN WERE INCLUDED IN HELL

The time when men were included in hell is recorded in the word (bible). It was in the word that a man (Eve) and another man (Adam) disobeyed God and ate of the forbidden fruit (evil of demons). It was in the word (bible) that a man (Adam and Eve) disobeyed God and ate of the tree of the knowledge of good and evil.

The Tree Of The Knowledge Of Good and Evil

As I (Jehovah) created all things, I discovered that I (Jehovah) am the God of all spirits (angels- light, angels- darkness, the god of darkness, Lucifer). As I (Jehovah) created all things, I discovered that I (Jehovah) am the God of all things (trees, birds, creeping things, cattle). As I (Jehovah) created all things, I(Jehovah) discovered that I am an impartial God. As I(Jehovah) created all things, I discovered I had not created the tree of the knowledge of good (holy) and evil. As I(Jehovah) created all things, I discovered I had not created the tree of life.

As I created all things, I discovered that the trees that were created were all living. As I created all things, I discovered if I had not created spirits (trees), I will be an impartial God. How can trees be called spirits? As I(Jehovah) walked into a region, I discovered that it will take men eternity to know mysteries especially from the third world. As I created all things, I discovered that the trees (spirits) would be against each other in time to come. As I created all things, I discovered that man would be created in time to come. As I created all things, I discovered that man would be called a living creature only if they represent the tree of life. As I created all things I discovered that man will be called a dead creature if they represent the tree of the knowledge of good and evil. As I (Jehovah) created all things, I discovered that the devil will seduce men to represent the tree of the knowledge of good and evil.

The Tree Of The Knowledge Of Good And Evil

As I (Jehovah) walked into a region (spiritually), I discovered that the region was neither of light nor of darkness. As I walked into a region (spiritually), I discovered that humanity will not know why I had to go into that region. As I (Jehovah) walked into a region, I discovered that the region was truly more of light than of darkness. As I (Jehovah) walked into a region, I discovered that the devil was already in that region.

The True Region of Light

As I (Jehovah) walked into a region of light, I discovered that truly it will not be good to create another tree (evil) seeing that the tree that was initially created was the tree of life although the tree was not to be mentioned, it was not just a tree that was created but a spirit (holy) that was made in the form of a tree to give Everlasting life to the saints.

The Creation of the Tree of Life

How can a spirit be created in the form of a tree if not that such a spirit is truly not to be in the presence of God but in the region where all souls (saints) will go to and pluck and eat. What is this region? What is this region? It is a region that was reserved by God for all souls (saints) to go and eat the fruit (mysteries) that will enable them to have the power (mysteries) to live forever to everlasting.

What is Everlasting

As I walked into a region, I discovered it was a region that the Creator will not want any to be. How can the Creator of heaven and earth create a place and placed a barrier to entering? It is a region that no one knows the end. How can a man (Jehovah) create a place for just himself and expect just himself to be there if not that the place is not an ordinary place but a place where all spirits were truly recloned. It is a place where spirits were recloned except himself. Yes! Except himself. How can God be in himself if not that he is a clone of himself? How can God be in himself if not that he is not to be called by just a name but a name?

What is the name?

He is Everlasting! He is not to be called by a name yet he has a name. He is what was written above (the mystery of the word-Everlasting). It is the name that cannot be called without thunder striking the sky.

Thunder

What is thunder? How can a man call his Creator by name? What is the name? What is the name? The name is Everlasting! Yes! He is Everlasting. His name is Everlasting but how can a man call his Creator by name.

THE NAME OF
THE CREATOR

The name of the Creator of all things is God. How can God be called God? The name of the Creator of all things is God. But how can God be called God? Yes! He is called God because he is the Creator of all things. But how can all things be created by God? Yes! That is why he is called God. Who called the name and why was the name called God?

God instituted that. Yes! He is the one that called himself God because he is God. How can a man call himself man because he is a man if not that it was God that created all things? How can God create all things when the devil is also created in a region that is beyond the reasoning of man? How can God create the devil when the devil was not just a beast (the evil of evil) but a thief? Yes! The devil is a thief, he stole man (Adam and Eve) at the Garden of Eden and man lost his place before God just like Lucifer lost his place before God.

Oh no! But how can God create the devil and allow him to regenerate into a serpent and deceive man at the Garden of Eden?

THE CREATION
OF THE DEVIL

Devil, how were you created? As I asked the question, I discovered that evil spirits were truly not evil initially but immediately the spirit of pride defeated Lucifer in paradise, evil spirits became evil. Evil spirits were once called the spirit of spirit before the fall of Lucifer because they were created by Jehovah in order to either chastise spirits and they were also created by Jehovah to show his great wealth. Jehovah is a man of wealth. He created all things for his glory both good and evil. Both holy and unholy. Both man and beast. Both angels and demons. Both...

The Creation - the Beginning of All Things

The devil was the one that made things evil the reason he is called the devil. He is not just an evil beast but he is a beast that is to be feared.

Who is the Beast?

The beast is the devil and the devil is the beast. The beast cannot be called the creation of God because the beast is truly not just a beast but a beast of beasts. He is not to be called just an ordinary beast because he was the one that made Jehovah reclone the last beast known as Satan because of the fall of man at the Garden of Eden. How can the devil make his Creator to almost weep (mystery) because of the fall of man?

THE FALL OF MAN

As I looked at the beginning of creation, I discovered that man should not have been created seeing that man was one of the weakest being created by God but so much loved (mysteries) by God. As I looked at the beginning of creation, I discovered that man was made up of clay and not just clay but a particle that was very very rare. The particle is known as the soulish particle which was used in cloning the soul. The soul cannot be said to have been created seeing it was not easy to create a soul from a particle but to clone a soul.

Yes! It is easy to create a man from clay and it is easier to create a man from stone but it is not easy to create a soul from clay. A soul is not a complete being but a soul can be complete if it has a spirit. A spirit is not a complete being but a spirit is complete when it has a soul. A soul and spirit make a being. But a soul that is polluted is not a complete being because when such a soul dies, the spirit will be a polluted spirit before Jehovah. A soul cannot die in the physical realm but a soul can die in the spiritual realm (spirit of spirit). A soul that is in hell is not a living soul but a dead soul. A soul that is in heaven (paradise) is a living soul but a soul that is in heaven cannot be a complete being too seeing such a soul has a spirit that is either before God (Jehovah) or before Spirit(Holy)

The Regeneration of Spirits

What is regeneration? Who knows what regeneration is all about? Regeneration is the ability of a soul to be cloned and a spirit entangled such a soul and a woman that is a month pregnant will be located and the entangled soul and spirit will transit from the third heaven into the earth and a woman that is a month pregnant will be located. The entangled soul and spirit will enter into her womb and the womb (heaven) will be a living womb.

Living Womb

A womb can be living and a womb can be dead (mysteries). A womb can be living and a womb can be dead. If a womb is living it means that the womb has a soul and Spirit(Holy) inside it. But when a womb (heaven) is dead, the womb has a soul and spirit(evil) inside it.

THE MYSTERY OF REGENERATION

A man was born as a drunkard but he later died and came back as an evangelist. How was that possible?

As I considered at the above question, I discovered that the most educated theologian on earth will not be able to answer such a question seeing that it is a mystery that is beyond man. As I looked at the question above, I discovered that even the best professor (flesh) on earth will not be able to answer such a question. As I looked at the question, I discovered that the best genius on earth will not be able to answer such a question. As I looked at the question, I discovered that humanity will not be able to answer the question. As I looked at the man (writer) writing, I discovered that it is not him (flesh) that is about to answer the question but a holy being that is in him. As I looked at the holy hands of the writer, I discovered that there were other hands (spiritually) writing through the writer. As I looked at the whites (men of knowledge), I discovered that they will not be able to discover the holy being writing through the writer using all their evil technology on earth. As I looked at the hand of the writer, I discovered that there was also another hand (holy) writing through the writer. As I looked at the pen of the writer, I discovered that it was not an ordinary pen but one that is highly spiritual. As I looked at the pen, I discovered that it is one that is highly spiritual. As I looked at the pen, I discovered that it was highly spiritual.

The Mystery of Regeneration

The question on the mystery of regeneration is one that is not easy to answer but will be answered by the power of the Holy Ghost.

The Answer

As I wanted to answer the question of regeneration, a being walked up to me and told me to remember that after death there is no repentance in the grave. As I looked at the being, I discovered he was not happy that God wanted to regenerate a man that just died in a ghastly accident.

The Great Mystery

As I looked at a man that just died, I discovered he died as a drunkard. As I looked at a man that just died, I discovered he was too (false) faithful to be before me after death. As I looked at him (drunkard), I discovered that he will weep for eternity in the pit (hell) if I don't help him. As I (Christ) looked at him, I discovered that he (drunkard) has a good heart but not a holy heart. As I (Christ) looked at the drunkard, I discovered he was told that it is appointed unto man once to die and after it is eternal judgment. As I (Christ) looked at the drunkard, I discovered that it will not be easy to regenerate (mysteries) him seeing he is having a polluted garment (mysteries) upon him. As I (Christ) looked at the drunkard, I discovered he was looking at the angels of judgment for mercy. As I (Christ) looked at the drunkard, I discovered that he was having a stain in between his legs. As I looked at the drunkard, I discovered he was jittering from head to toe seeing he had seen how the mighty wind (angel of darkness) was blowing souls from the region of light to that of darkness. As I (Christ) looked at the drunkard, I discovered he was not interested in what was happening with the souls that were before him but on the way the wind (the angel of darkness) was blowing damned souls into the pit (hell). As I (Christ) looked at him (drunkard), I discovered that he was the only one that the devil wanted to reclone.

Recloning of the Dead

I (Jehovah) created the devil and I created Lucifer. I created the devil but Lucifer was the one that disappointed himself after pride (spirit) defeated him in paradise. As I (Jehovah) looked at the devil, I (ehovah) discovered he (the devil) was too evil to be called the creation of God. As I (Jehovah) looked at Satan, I (Jehovah) discovered that it will take the whole of eternity to know how I created Satan.

The Creation of Satan

How can a man say that there is just one (evil being) that is tormenting humanity? How can a man say there is just one tormenting humanity? As I (Jehovah) looked at the creation of Satan, I discovered that any man that misses heaven will want to know if Jehovah is truly the one that created what is tormenting them in the pit (hell). As I looked into the pit (hell), I discovered there was just one being there and that being is Satan.

Satan

Satan, I (Christ) rebuke you! How can you be this heartless seeing that I (Jehovah) created humanity with a very, very rare particle (soul) and now you are destroying that particle inside your apartment (hell)?

DESTROYING THE SOUL PARTICLE IN HELL

How can a man (damned) die? How can a man (damned) die? As I (Christ) asked the question, I discovered that many (damned) that were in the pit (hell) would want to die (mysteries out of mysteries). How can the soul particle be destroyed? How can the soul particles be destroyed?

Destroying of the Soul Particles

The soul particles can only be destroyed in the lake. How can souls (damned) in hell believe (impossible) that they will die again immediately they fall into the pit (hell)? How can a drunkard (damned) that died as a drunkard believe that he will be given a second chance if not that God is just too merciful and his mercy endures forever? How can a masturbator that died believe that he (she) will die again after being thrown into the pit? Finally, how can a false pastor that died as a liar (deceiving the sheepfold) die again after being thrown into the pit (hell)?

As I looked at a man (drunkard) that was about to be blown into the pit(hell), I (Christ) discovered that he will not eat again except I help him. As I looked at him, I discovered that the devil wants to reclone the man should he be thrown into the pit (hell). As I looked at the man (drunkard), I discovered that it was truly appointed unto man once to die and after it was judgment. As I (Christ) looked at that part of my word (the bible), I discovered that the whole world will never, never beliEve that a man who just died and his body is burnt in a ghastly accident could be born again through regeneration by the power of the Holy Ghost. Yes! It is impossible with man (mortals) but not with God.

REGENERATION OF THE DEAD

Regeneration is not an ordinary mystery that would be easily taught to man but by the power of the Holy Ghost. Yes! It will take man eternity to believe that a man (drunkard) would die and be reborn as an evangelist.

The mystery

A man (drunkard) dies and is about to be blown into the pit (hell) and the devil was patiently waiting for the man seeing the man was saved through a holy angel severally especially from poisons by his fellow drunkards. And because of that, the devil wanted to regenerate the inward being of the man (drunkard). As I (Christ) looked at the man (drunkard), I discovered that he will not eat again if he were to be blown into the pit (hell). As I looked at him, I discovered that the devil wanted to regenerate him.

Regeneration of the Dead By the Devil

The devil also regenerates the dead especially those that died as sinners even after God had saved them several times (mysteries) through his holy angels. As I (Christ) looked at a man (sinner) that just died, I discovered that the devil already had his clone.

The Clone of the Dead

The clone of the dead is an exact replication of a man that is living (filthy) in sin. The devil has exact copies (the evil of demon) of sinners on earth and with that, he controls (the evil of demons) them to do his evil bidding. How can a man (sinner) wake up one morning and all that enters into his mind is on how to look for a rope and commit suicide? How can a man (sinner) wake up one morning and all that enters his mind is on how to rape a woman? How can a man (sinner) wake up one morning and all that enters his mind is on how to fornicate with a woman that is not his wife? How can a woman (harlot) wake up one morning and all that enters her mind is on how she will leave her matrimonial bed and begin to sleep around on other beds? How can a woman (harlot) wake up one morning and all that enters her mind is on how to insert her fingers into her genital just to masturbate herself? How can a woman (harlot) use her vaginal fluid as rituals (prostitution) to make money? How can a woman (harlot) look at films (pornography) just to satisfy her flesh? How can a woman (harlot) sleep with more than a man upon the bed? As I (Christ) looked at the creation of God, tears of blood trickled down my chin. Humanity is very foolish.

The Clones of the Dead

Once a man (sinner) dies in sin the devil already has such a clone. The clone of sinners is just a replication of the inside being of the sinner.

The Clone

A man was a virgin and immediately the man starts watching pornography, the devil regenerates a clone that looks very much like him. As I (Christ) looked at the man who was once a virgin, I discovered he did not know that the devil has cheated him. Yes! The devil had cheated him seeing the devil will now be controlling him at will. The devil will not just control him at will but the devil also has a clone of his genital organ and with that, he will be stimulated by the devil to always fornicate.

Fornicators

As I (Christ) looked at men (flesh), I discovered they were just too foolish not to know that immediately a man (woman) fornicates, the devil already has the clone of his genital organ and with that, the devil will be controlling the person at will. Fornicators are the most foolish human beings on earth.

The Effect of Fornication

How can a man seat before television and expect the devil to spare him from seducing him either into masturbating or fornication?

Effects of Television

As I (Christ) looked at what the devil brought into the world through the whites (men of knowledge), tears of blood trickled down my chin. As I (Christ) looked at the object (television), I discovered that humans are just too foolish not to know that I created two trees (spirits) in the middle of the Garden of Eden. The tree of life (holy) and the tree of the knowledge of good and evil (the unholy).

As I (Christ) looked at the tree at the middle of Eden, I discovered that man was truly foolish seeing that once a man (flesh) eats the fruit (the evil of demon), man will not just die but man will also know good and evil which signifies evil. Yes! The tree of the knowledge of good and evil is a tree that was created by God but it was not of God because God (Jehovah) created the tree (spirit) so that evil will also have its place before God (Jehovah) seeing that Jehovah is the God of light (holy) and darkness (evil). How can God (Jehovah) create a tree (spirit) and the devil made man (Adam and Eve) eat (the evil of demons) from that evil tree.

The Tree of the Knowledge Of Good and Evil

The tree of the knowledge of good and evil was a tree that cannot be seen without looking at it the second time. The tree of the knowledge of good and evil was a tree that was most attractive to the eyes (flesh) yet it was just too evil to go close to it. The tree of the knowledge of good and evil is a tree that Lucifer in all his glory cannot be compared to the glory that was physically seen on that tree. The tree of the knowledge of good and evil is a spirit that was created by the Creator (Jehovah) to be away from the presence of God.

THE MYSTERY SO FAR

A man was born an evangelist but he died as a drunkard. A man was born an evangelist but he truly died a drunkard. How is this possible? A man after living in the filthiness of the flesh died as a drunkard but as he was going before the throne of judgment, there was a decision from the throne of God for the man to be regenerated. Regeneration is the ability of a soul, either holy or polluted, to be recloned and the clone is entangled to either the spirit(holy) or spirit(evil) and a normal baby or an evil baby is born.

Evil Children

An evil child is one that the cloned soul is entangled to a spirit(evil).

Evil Spirit

Spirit(evil) is entirely different from evil spirits created by Jehovah. Spirit(evil) is the spirit (breath of God) in man that died and did not make heaven but the spirit (evil) did not return to the Creator but is living with men on earth. Humanity did not know they are living with several millions of spirits(evil). Evil spirits are at the darkest region of darkness while millions are on earth going around with women (fornicators, sometimes masturbators) to tie a physical man that will sleep with such a woman. Evil spirits are five hundred and fifty times more wicked than demons. Evil spirits are five hundred and fifty times more dangerous than demons. Evil spirits had been in existence before Lucifer was created.

The genesis of all this is the fall of man at the Garden of Eden.

The Fall of Man

Man, do you know what you did to me (Jehovah)? Do you know what you caused? Do you know if you had not fallen, death (spirit of spirits) wouldn't have reigned? Do you know if you had not fallen it is only Lucifer, devil and his agents (fallen angels) would have been in the pit (hell)?

Regeneration of Things By Jehovah

How can mortal men believe that I (Jehovah) created things out of nothing (impossible)? How can man believe that I (Jehovah) created the whole world out of nothing (very impossible)?

The Creation of All Things

I (Jehovah) have a clone (Jesus) my clone has a clone (the Holy Ghost). I (Jehovah) have a clone (Jesus) and I have many clones (holy spirits). My clone (Jesus) has just one clone (the Holy Ghost). The clone (Holy Ghost) cannot have another clone (impossibilities). Lucifer has a clone (the devil), the clone (devil) has a clone (Satan). If I (Jehovah) ask men (flesh) a question, they will not be able to answer me (Jehovah).

THE QUESTION

What is the difference between the Holy Ghost and holy spirit(s)? What is the difference between Jehovah and Jesus? What is the difference between the spirit of the dead and an evil spirit? What is the difference between a normal child and an evil child?

As I looked at the questions above, I discovered it is truly not a question but a mystery.

The Mysteries

How can I (Jehovah) and my clone (Jesus) be one if not in terms of love?

The Love of the Trinity

As I (Jehovah) looked at men (flesh), I discovered they were confused about the mystery of the Trinity. The mystery of the Trinity has been explained in plain language by the writer in a book titled "the battle of life".

As I (Jehovah) looked at the world, I discovered men (flesh) were truly confused both in knowledge and in wisdom (refined-bible). Yes! Men (flesh) are truly confused. As I (Jehovah) looked at men (flesh), I discovered that men does not know that I (Christ) and my Father (Jehovah) are one in terms (mysteries) of love and only love.

The Power of the Trinity

The power of the trinity is the power of the Father . The power of the Trinity is the power of the Son . The power of the Trinity is the power of the Holy Ghost. The power of the Holy Ghost is not the power of Jehovah. The power of Jehovah is not the power of the Son. The power of the Son is not the power of the Holy Ghost.

The Power of the Father

The power of the Father (Jehovah) is the power with which he created all things. The power of the Father (Jehovah) is the power with which he created spirits. The power of Jehovah is the power with which he created the universe. The power of Jehovah is the power with which he created merman and mermaid. The power of Jehovah is the power with which he cloned spirits and spirits of spirits.

Cloning of Spirits

How can spirits be said to have been created? As I looked at the beginning of creation, I discovered that spirits were all cloned and recloned at different layers. Lucifer was not just cloned but was recloned after he fell and became the devil. The cloning of spirits is a mystery that will not be written in this book because of a mystery which is beyond the explanation of the writer although God (Jehovah) is the real Author using mortal man (flesh) to write.

The Power of the Son (Jesus)

The power of the Son is the power with which he (Christ) created humanity. The power of the Son (Christ) is the power with which he (Christ) said "let there be light" and there was light. The power of the Son (Christ) is the power with which he separated light from darkness. The power of the Son (Christ) is the power with which he commanded day to night and night to day. The power of the Son(Christ) is the power with which he called man (clay) from the dust.

The Power of the Holy Ghost

The power of the Holy Ghost is the power that parted the red sea. The power of the Holy Ghost is the power that kept the Son (Christ) for forty days and night in the wilderness without food and water . The power of the Holy Ghost is the power that destroyed Satan in the pit (hell). The power of the Holy Ghost is the power that makes thunder to strike in the cloud. The power of the Holy Ghost is the power that caused the devil to run whenever Jehovah is angry (holy) . The power of the Holy Ghost is the power that destroys the occultic world from becoming rampant here and there on earth. The power of the Holy Ghost is the power that will make humanity fear during the rapture. The power of the Holy Ghost is the power that will make the ocean roar during the rapture . The power of the Holy Ghost is the power that will make sinners to fear at the pit (hell). The power of the Holy Ghost is the power that will make other false religion on earth tremble during the rapture.

THE RAPTURE

How can man born of a woman understand the rapture in plain language? How can a man born of a woman understand the mystery of the rapture? How can a man born of a woman explain the rapture through his knowledge(filthy)?

As I looked into the bible, I discovered that the book of Revelation will be explained in plain language by the power of the Holy Ghost by a man (half human, half spirit). How can a man born of a woman explain the mystery of the rapture embedded in the book of Revelation if not that such a man (half human, half spirit) has been sealed by the power of the Holy Ghost to explain the mystery of the rapture in plain language. As I looked at men, I discovered that it will take the whites (men of knowledge) eternity to explain why a man that was covered with flesh cannot be an ordinary man.

The Writer

The mystery of the creation of the writer has been explained in plain language in a book titled " the thunder of God". How can a man born of a woman see (mysteries) the Holy Ghost eye (spirit of spirits) to eye (spirits) if not that that man was supernaturally created.

The Supernatural Creation of the Writer

As I (Christ) looked at a man (the writer), I discovered that it will take mortal men the whole of eternity to understand who the writer was.

The Man (Writer)

The writer is not an ordinary human being . The writer is spirit. The writer is spirit. The writer is spirit.

Spirit

The spirit of the writer is not an ordinary spirit (breath of God). The spirit of the writer is not an ordinary spirit (breath of Jehovah). The spirit of the writer is not an ordinary spirit (holy).

What is the Spirit

The spirit of the writer is not an ordinary spirit.

Ordinary Spirit

Spirits of men (flesh) were cloned at a region that is not to be mentioned. The spirit of man is not just the breath of God but the breath of spirit (holy). The spirit of God is holy and the spirit of the Son is the Holy Ghost. The spirit of the Son cannot be inside the cloned souls of men but the spirits (holy) of the Father (Jehovah) can be in the cloned souls of men.

Cloned Spirits

Cloned spirits are not ordinary spirits. Cloned spirits are spirits that can function (mysteries of mysteries) on their own. They are spirits that cannot be easily chained by men (evil men/cultists).

Cultists

How can a man (cloned spirit) be initiated by evil men (cultists) if not that they are very, very foolish? As I (Christ) looked at a man (the writer), I (Christ) discovered that many occultic societies in the world, including the devil, have tried all their possible best (the evil of demon) to initiate the writer.

The Devil

How can the devil also assist cultists in helping to initiate a man (the writer) if not that he was supernaturally created?

THE MYSTERY OF THE RAPTURE

The mystery of the rapture is not ordinary but would be explained in plain language by the help of the Holy Ghost. The rapture is the ability (mysteries of mysteries) of God (the Trinity) to take away the saved either by death or by a way that theologian only know.

The Way that Theologians Know

How can God sound (mysteries of mysteries) his trumpet and only those that their name is in the lamb's book of life will be taken away mysteriously to be with God (Christ) and the holy God in the cloud (a thousand years). Yes! It is very impossible with man (sinner) but not with God.

The mystery

Once trumpet sounds, an angel(wind) will be sent on earth to rapture the saved. Once trumpet sounds on earth, another angel will be sent to release the dragon(Satan). Once the trumpet sounds, an angel will be sent to close the book of life. Once the trumpet sounds, an angel will be sent to prepare the hall (mysteries) for welcoming the saved for a thousand years, once the trumpet sounds.

Another Mystery

Once the trumpet sounds, the dead in Christ will be blown into the pit(hell). No, Mr writer, how can the dead in Christ be blown into the pit (hell)? You are very wrong!

I Am Not Wrong

You are truly not wrong because you are not the one writing but had it mean you are the one (flesh) writing from your knowledge (filthy) through the bible, I would have torn this your holy literature I am reading.

Okay! Prove yourself correct and I (reader) will read all your books

The Proof

Elijah was taken to heaven but Elijah is here on earth. Elijah was taken to heaven but Elijah is still living here on earth.

How?

Okay! A prophet cannot be said to be an ordinary man. If that prophet is truly a prophet ordained by God in the womb. Yes! A prophet ordained in the womb is a prophet that knows he is going to die and make himself very prepared before his death. A prophet that does not know that he is going to die is not just a foolish prophet but an unholy prophet.

The Prophets

Prophets are not ordinary humans. Prophets are specially created by Jehovah to chain the devil through his act (evil of evil) on man.

Prophets are supernaturally created by the Creator (Jehovah). Man is specially created by the Creator (Christ). Beasts (animals, etc) are specially created by the Creator (Holy Ghost).

As I (Christ) looked at men (mortals), I discovered they were just too confused about the rapture although many theologians have tried to explain the mystery of the rapture through their knowledge(filthy) using my word (the bible).

As I (Christ) looked at a man(writer), I discovered he does not know what will happen immediately I (Christ) sound my trumpet but he has a little idea from a few he has been written from his books. Okay! Mr writer you are about to explain the mystery that a billion professors (flesh) put together for a billion years would not be able to explain.

Explanation of the Rapture

Who are the dead in Christ? Who are the dead in Christ? The dead in Christ are those that died but were not allowed to see God.

Those that Died But Were Not Allowed to See God

How can a man (sinner) die in Christ? How can a man (sinner) die in Christ? As I looked at my word (the bible), I discovered that many have gotten it wrong, they are using their filthy knowledge to explain my word (the bible) which is highly spiritual although written literally.

As I (Christ) looked at a man (a drunkard) that died recently, I discovered that he died in sin (devil) although he was born into a Christian home. As I (Christ) looked at him, I discovered that he was too foolish not to know that he died in Christ seeing he was told about Jesus but he repudiated the saving grace of God on his life. As I (Christ) looked at him, I discovered that he was about to be judged seeing that he had already been judged before his death.

As I (Christ) looked at him, I discovered that he was too faithful to be called a damned soul(false) seeing he was too fond of me (Christ). As I (Christ) looked at him (drunkard), I discovered he was about to be blown into the region of darkness seeing he was also too faithful to be blown into the pit (hell). As I (Christ) looked at him, I discovered that he was jittering from head to toe as he was told that where he will be going is a place that is meant for the devil and his agent. As I (Christ) looked at him, I discovered that he was about to plead for mercy (impossible); mercy and repentance are only available on earth except if I want to turn the person back to his body or if the body is burnt then to regenerate him into a woman that is a month pregnant.

As I (Christ) looked at my word (the bible), I discovered that theologians will never, never believe that those that are the dead in Christ are truly those that were once warned of the wrath to come but heard and repudiated the saving grace.

It is finished! It is finished!